AMIGO

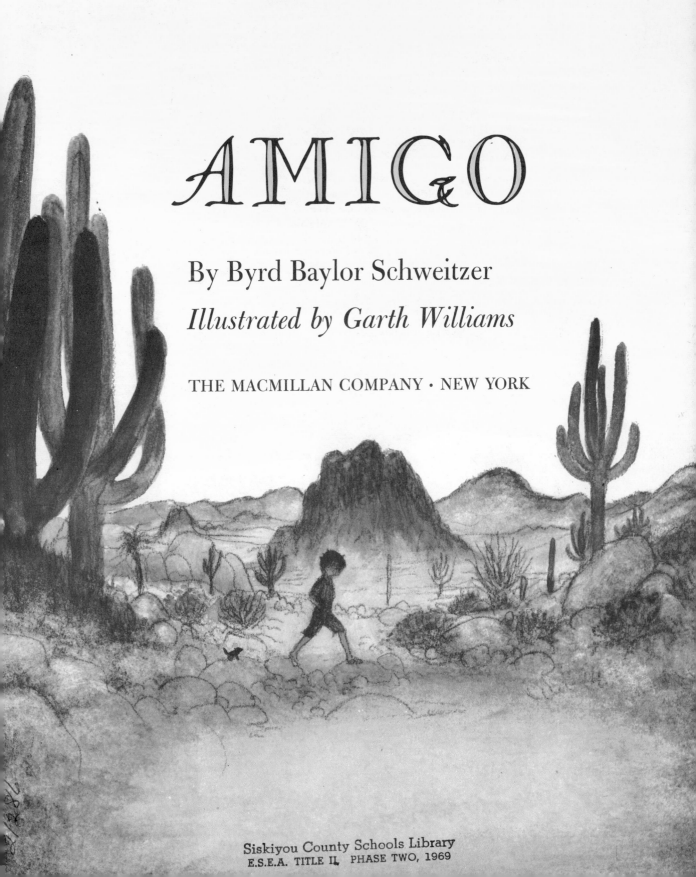

AMIGO

By Byrd Baylor Schweitzer

Illustrated by Garth Williams

THE MACMILLAN COMPANY · NEW YORK

Library of Congress catalog card number: 63-18124

The Macmillan Company, New York
Collier-Macmillan Canada, Ltd., Toronto, Ontario

Printed in the United States of America

Fourth Printing, 1966

For George and Libby Baylor

His mother said,
"Come, Francisco, my son.
Tell me why your eyes are sad,
My little one."

His father said,
"How quiet you are.
Let me play you a tune
On my old guitar."

Plink.
Plink.
He strums the guitar,
Singing,
"Troubles run.
Fast and far . . .
Past the mountains
Behind a star."
Plink.
Plink.
A-plink.

. 1 .

Francisco listened to the song.
Then he told them what was wrong.

"You know, I want a dog. Any dog. A hound . . .
A dog I'll call Amigo and he'll follow me around
Wherever I go. Wherever I go
He'll be there.
Some days I'll follow him
Just to make it fair."

Francisco's mother turned with a sigh.
Francisco's father looked off at the sky.
"No, Francisco. It's all we can do
Just trying to feed your brothers and you."

Francisco seldom thought about
The things he had to do without
Because
He thought about the things he had.
In his mind he tried to add them up . . .
So many brothers.
So many jokes.
So many miles of desert all around.
So many cactuses. So many mountains—
So many places where caves can be found.
And
Plenty of wishes
To wish on a star.
Plenty of songs
In that guitar,
But
Not enough money in his father's pocket—
That's the way things are.

Francisco's father mines for gold.
He knows he'll find it before he's old,
But
He hasn't found it yet
So he has to say,
"No, Francisco.
Another mouth to feed
Is one more than I need.
You just forget
About a pet."
His mother asked,
"What's small and wild
And can feed itself?
We'll have that, my child."

"But *what?*" Francisco frowned.

"You could tame a bird,
A bright wild bird
With the sweetest song
You ever heard."

"No. No. I can't fly.
He could go much
Higher than I."

"Up in the mountains
There are wildcats.
You can catch one if you're bold.
Here in the valley
There are tortoises one hundred years old."

"A tortoise is too slow for my fast feet,
And wildcats won't play in the desert heat."

"How about a lizard?
How about a quail?
How about a coyote
With a yellow tail?"

"No. No. And I don't want a frog."
Francisco shook his head,
He had to have a dog.

Suddenly his mother whirled around.
Her voice came out with a laughing sound.
"Ah, Francisco, my son!
A PRAIRIE DOG!
Could that be the one?"

They all laughed.
"A PRAIRIE DOG."
It seemed so funny—
He's more like a ground squirrel
Or a mouse or a bunny
Than a dog . . .
A strange little creature
With fast little feet,
Who doesn't mind
The desert heat.

"A prairie dog would be easy to find.
Of course, I had a *real* dog in my mind
But
If I try
I think that I
Could love
A prairie dog . . .
A tiny black-eyed, run-around
Hole-in-the-ground
Squeak-a-dry-sound
Prairie dog,
A very
Merry
Prairie
Dog."

Francisco's father said,
"You'd have to win his love
Before you tame him."

"Yes, I will win his love.
Then I will name him
Amigo.
That's the name I was saving
For some big hound—
But I think it will do
For a little run-around."

His mother smiled.
"How do you tame a prairie dog,
A thing that's wild?
How do you make him walk beside
A human child?"

"I'll give him presents
Like water and seeds
And tall sweet weeds.
I'll give him love
And whatever he needs."

Francisco hurried
To Prairie-Dog Town.
Very quietly
He sat down
On a rocky slope
To watch and wait
And dream and hope.

Prairie-Dog Town is a town under ground,
All tunnel and burrow and hilly mound . . .
The busiest town for miles around.
Ten little heads popped out of the earth
And looked around curiously
And jabbered furiously
And frowned at Francisco for all they were worth.

He wanted them to know that he
Was a friend, a brother,
Wanted them to see him
Simply as another
Desert creature
Who meant no harm.
So he lay down
With his head on his arm.
The sun was warm.
He nestled deep
Into clumps of grass.
Time passed. And then,
Francisco fell asleep.

When he opened his eyes
There wasn't a sound.
He sat up
And looked around
And found
One prairie dog still sitting in his place.
He seemed to be studying Francisco's face.

"Can that be Amigo?
Does he read my mind?
Does he know he's the one
That I came to find?"

Very gently he whispered
"Amigo . . ."
The word
Was so soft
It could only be heard
By one prairie dog
And one low-flying bird . . .
"Amigo . . ."
It was half laugh, half song,
The kind of word that floats along.

That day wherever Francisco went
He went with his dreams and he went content.
And he went with a hop and he went with a hope
And he jumped over rocks like an antelope.

Now you know Francisco
And the way he planned
To tame him a friend
In that desert land.
But you still don't know—
Though you very soon will—
What creature was hiding
Behind that hill . . .

Look
Toward the mountain,
There
Toward the sun.
See that brown speck
Dart and run?

That is Amigo.

The desert is wide
And the rocks are tall.
You might not notice
A creature so small.
But that is Amigo,
The prairie-dog child
Who runs with the wind
When the wind runs wild.

Just one summer old,
Adventurous and bold,
He's small enough to look
A tortoise in the eye,
Or exchange remarks
With a passing fly,
And brave enough to jump
At stars in the sky—
He never really caught one
But he likes to try.

Yes, this is Amigo . . .
Always full of ideas,
Saying summer is *his*—
And maybe it is—
To run through.

But should he be running
So fast and so far?
Why isn't he home
Where his brothers are,
In the dim burrows
Which wind far down
Below the surface
Of Prairie-Dog Town?

There
Old prairie dogs sit in the sun
Keeping watch through the summer day
While the little ones dodge in and out
Like children at play.

But Amigo isn't there.
He's *everywhere,*
Following every path he knows.
He doesn't worry,
He only *goes* . . .

And where is he going?
What does he seek?
Why does he gaze
At the mountain peak?

Amigo runs to a certain hill.
There he stops and waits until
He hears the sound of a boy's easy laughter.
Then he knows he's found what he came after:
That boy!

Amigo sits,
Quiet as a stone,
And sees the boy
Walking alone
And carrying a heavy pail
Of water down the rocky trail
And singing.
Ah, what a sound!
Amigo found
It going round
His head all day.
It would not go away—
That sound of singing,
Ringing
In his head.

He said,
"I know every sound for miles around,
Every small and quiet sound—
Like earthworms walking underground
And the whisper of quail
And the wet creaking wail
Of baby toads after a rain,
And the rustle of grass
Where a deer has lain.
Yes,
I think there's many a sound
Pleasant enough to have around.

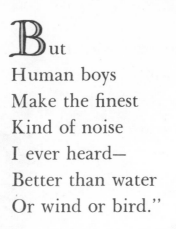

But
Human boys
Make the finest
Kind of noise
I ever heard—
Better than water
Or wind or bird.''

This boy was a little thing—
Only so high.
But he seemed to Amigo
To reach the sky,
Tall as a mountain,
Brown and strong.
Amigo followed him
All day long.

He heard his whistle
And he heard his song
Carried by the wind,
Light as a feather.

Amigo said,
"I wonder whether
He ever saw me
Peeping from under
That mesquite tree
And popping up
From clumps of grass
Along the way
To see him pass."

But his mother said,
"Be careful, my child.
A human boy
Is very wild."

Amigo said,
"I'll tame him if it takes a year.
The sound of that boy is all I want to hear!"

"You can't mean that!
Better go play with the
Old pack rat."

The prairie dogs listened
With great surprise.
You could tell what they thought
By the look in their eyes.

One finally said, as he gazed at the sun,
"Better learn from those who are wise, little one.
Mountain is your friend.
Wind is your toy.
Let's stop this talk about
A human boy."

A hundred aunts, uncles and cousins agreed.
"That's right," they said,
And they wiggled their whiskers
And nodded their heads.
"Oh, yes, that's right," they said.
"That's right."

But Amigo told them,
"He doesn't look wild.
I know if I try
I can tame that child."

"How about an ant?"

"An ant?
I can't
Love an ant.
I just can't."

"How about a bee
With a lazy buzz?"

"No. I don't like honey
And he does."

"Play with a cricket.
Play with a quail.
Tame you a lizard
With a sandy tail."

"They're all good friends
But they're just not boys
And they can't make
That fine boy-noise."

Amigo tried to make them understand.
"I'm as much a part of the desert land
As any mountain or grain of sand,
Or soft quail cry
Or sunset sky
Or dust-devil blowing high
As a bird.
And that boy
Is a part of it too—
The same as I.
He's a desert thing like any other.
Sometimes I think he is my brother."

Amigo's mother nodded her head.
"Taming a boy seems odd," she said.
"It's never been done, as far as I know,
But no one ever loved one so—
And that makes all the difference.
You may be the one
Who will do it, my son."

.30.

"The thing to do now
Is tame him.
But how?
What can I give him?
I wish I knew.
I have no treasures,
Not even a few."

"Just give him something
That pleases you."

"Like silvery sand
To hold in his hand?
Or the blue jay feather
That floated down
Straight from the sky
To Prairie-Dog Town?
Or that cool green shadowy grass
Which grows so tall at the mountain pass
And tastes of mountain water?"

His mother said, "These
Would surely please
A boy."

So Amigo scampered
And ran and hopped.
The sun was high
Before he stopped—
At the very top
Of the mountain pass,
Where all the grass
Was sweet as honey
And tall enough to hide in.
Amigo took great pride in
His work that day.

. 31 .

He sniffed a thousand blades of grass
Before he found the one
That smelled the most like mountain water—
And shone like mountain sun.

He took the green blade
Tenderly down
Into the valley near
Prairie-Dog Town.
And beside the path
Where the boy often came,
He placed the grass on a small white stone—
Which he always thought of
As his own.

As he waited he made a kind of game
Of dreaming the boy was already tame
And knew his name—
And said,
"Amigo."

But it was no game,
For the boy came along
Trailing his song
In the windy air.
And it was no dream,
For he saw Amigo there.
He did not speak.
He only sat
Very quietly gazing at
The world of sun and sand.
And when he left, a blade of grass
Was clutched in his brown hand.

. 34 .

And Amigo ran home
Bounding with joy,
Shouting, "Listen,
I've just about
Tamed me a boy!"

At the same time,
On the same day,
You could hear
Francisco say,
"Mama, I know that he's
Just about mine!
Isn't that wonderful?
Isn't that fine?"

Francisco went back to the stone
Every day.
He was a friend
In every way.
He brought wild cherries
Gathered in the mountains
And fat dark berries
That grew on sandy banks.
To see Amigo eat them
Was all the thanks
He needed.
When the summer sun beat fiercely down
And the heat lay heavy on Prairie-Dog Town,
He found a rock shaped like a cup
And every morning he filled it up
With water.

And he kept one eye on the sky
To warn Amigo when hawks flew by.
And every day
Amigo came closer
To the place
Where Francisco sat—
As near as that.

The boy was taming Amigo.
Oh, yes,
That's so.
And if you were watching Amigo
You'd know
That he was taming Francisco.
And you would think
The boy wished he were tame
The way he came
Closer
And
Closer.

Francisco took the presents
Amigo left here and there.
He even stuck that blue jay
Feather in his hair.

Many a time
The boy would lie down
In the tall wispy grass
Near Prairie-Dog Town,
Quiet as a field mouse in its nest,
Like any desert creature taking a rest.
Amigo liked knowing that he was near.
He listened for his whistle in the summer air—
And sure enough the whistle was there!

Amigo ran
Close to the sound.
Francisco smiled,
Turned around
And met Amigo.

That was the way
It happened that day.
First they climbed a hill.
They followed a bee.
Then they stopped to rest
By a mesquite tree.
They didn't talk much for the wind was shrill.
They sat there quietly, as good friends will,
Admiring the view from that rocky hill.

Now
Francisco thought,
"I've tamed me a prairie dog.
He's my greatest joy."
And
Amigo thought,
"Mine is the *best* pet.
I've tamed me a boy."

Amigo squeaked a happy sound,   . *41* .
And when he was through
Francisco said, "Yes,
I think so too."